Huge big tall tree

Uncle Wiggily's hollow stump bungalow

Auto garage

Airship garage

Road to the seashore

Woodland Path

Post office

NO ADMITTANCE

Airship

Water tub

old dead tree

Cracked rock

Muskrat house

Frog pond

Dam

Uncle Wiggily's Happy Days

Abridged Edition

By Howard R. Garis

Illustrated by

Aldren Watson

Platt & Munk, Publishers/New York
A Division of Grosset & Dunlap

To
Boys And Girls
Everywhere

Dear Children:

Uncle Wiggily has asked me to tell you that this is a new book about his latest adventures; the first new book in a long time. The jolly old rabbit gentleman with the pink, twinkling nose, calls this book his "HAPPY DAYS."

In this book you may read how Uncle Wiggily went adventuring in his automobile with the bologna sausage wheels; how he played a trick on the Bad Chaps and then how he sailed off in his funny airship.

I spent many happy days writing about Uncle Wiggily's adventures in this book.

I hope you boys and girls may have happy days reading about them.

Uncle Wiggily also hopes you will enjoy hearing of the many strange events that happened during his Happy Days.

Uncle Wiggily and I send you greetings and best wishes.

Your friend,

Howard R. Garis

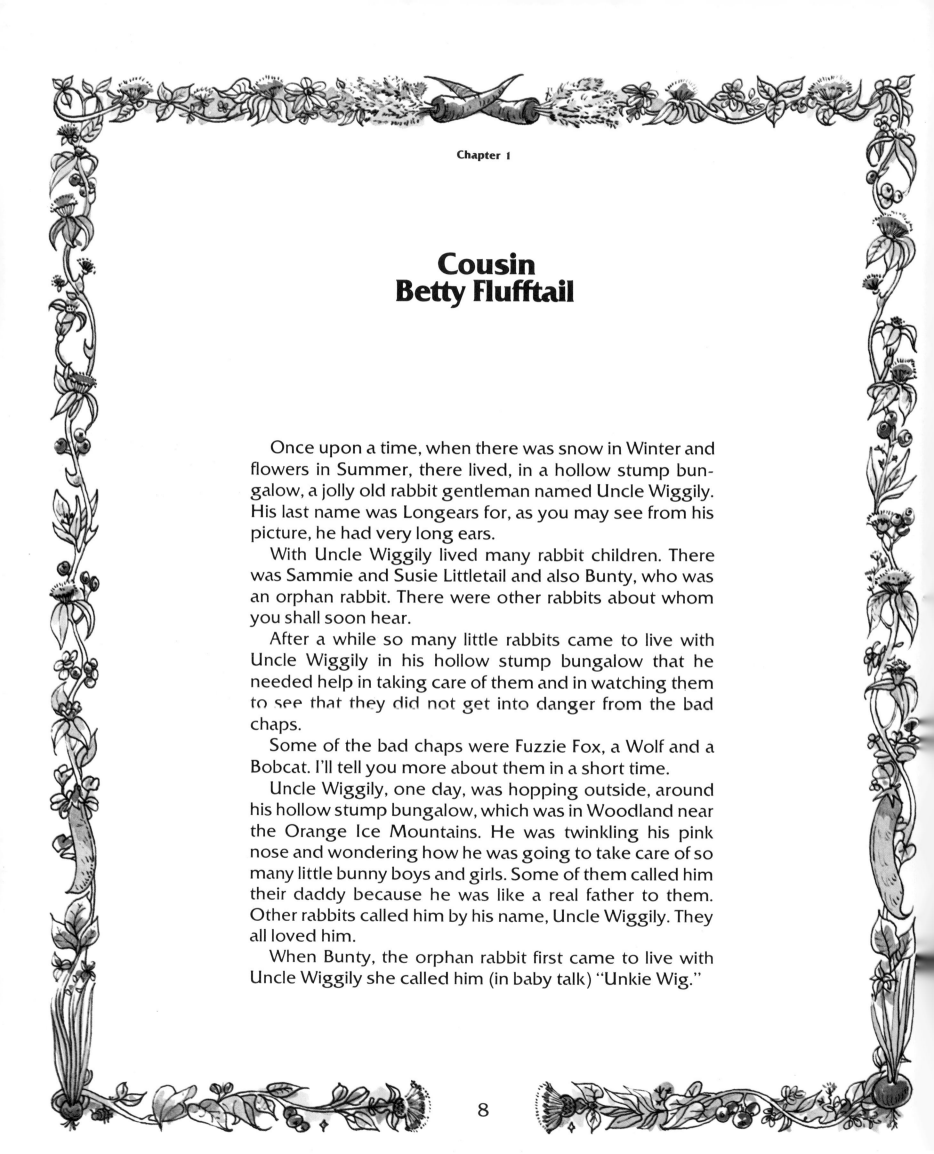

Chapter 1

Cousin Betty Flufftail

Once upon a time, when there was snow in Winter and flowers in Summer, there lived, in a hollow stump bungalow, a jolly old rabbit gentleman named Uncle Wiggily. His last name was Longears for, as you may see from his picture, he had very long ears.

With Uncle Wiggily lived many rabbit children. There was Sammie and Susie Littletail and also Bunty, who was an orphan rabbit. There were other rabbits about whom you shall soon hear.

After a while so many little rabbits came to live with Uncle Wiggily in his hollow stump bungalow that he needed help in taking care of them and in watching them to see that they did not get into danger from the bad chaps.

Some of the bad chaps were Fuzzie Fox, a Wolf and a Bobcat. I'll tell you more about them in a short time.

Uncle Wiggily, one day, was hopping outside, around his hollow stump bungalow, which was in Woodland near the Orange Ice Mountains. He was twinkling his pink nose and wondering how he was going to take care of so many little bunny boys and girls. Some of them called him their daddy because he was like a real father to them. Other rabbits called him by his name, Uncle Wiggily. They all loved him.

When Bunty, the orphan rabbit first came to live with Uncle Wiggily she called him (in baby talk) "Unkie Wig."

But after Bunty grew up and passed out of Kindergarten class she was not allowed to use any more baby talk. But once in a while she would forget and call him "Unkie Wig."

"I don't know what I am going to do if any more little rabbits come to live with me," said Uncle Wiggily one day. He was sort of talking out loud to himself, when, all of a sudden, a voice called from the frog pond:

"I would like to help you take care of the little rabbits," said the voice.

"Who are you?" asked Uncle Wiggily.

"I am Nurse Jane Fuzzy Wuzzy and I am a muskrat lady," went on the voice. Out of the frog pond climbed the muskrat lady, her fur all sleek and shining with water. She had on a bathing suit. "I will come and live with you and be your housekeeper," said Nurse Jane who had a squeaky voice and a long tail.

"Then please come," invited Uncle Wiggily. "I have so many little rabbit children living with me now that I don't know what to do. It keeps me busy just making carrot sandwiches for them."

She went into her house, took off her bathing suit, put on a dress with a long apron, packed her birch bark valise with some extra clothes and hurried away.

Nurse Jane soon reached Uncle Wiggily's hollow stump bungalow and at once began housekeeping for him and the many little rabbit children. They loved the jolly rabbit gentleman with the pink twinkling nose so much that they never wanted to leave him.

The jolly old rabbit gentleman was glad to have the muskrat lady for his housekeeper.

"I can have more time for adventures, now," he said. "I shall spend happy days having adventures." And he did.

But, as time went on, more rabbits came to live with Uncle Wiggily so that he and Nurse Jane were kept very busy. Sometimes Uncle Wiggily could not find time to go adventuring.

"I declare, I don't know what to do," said Uncle Wiggily one day to Uncle Butter, a goat gentleman.

"Why don't you ask your Cousin Betty Flufftail to help you?" suggested Uncle Butter.

"Cousin Betty Flufftail ho, hum! I never thought of her," said Uncle Wiggily. "I believe that would be a fine idea. I'll hop over to her burrow and ask her."

Cousin Betty Flufftail was an old lady rabbit who lived in a house under the ground, called a burrow. It wasn't far from Uncle Wiggily's hollow stump bungalow. Cousin Betty had a little bunch of fur for a tail. It was fluffy and wobbled up and down.

So that's how she came to live in the hollow stump bungalow so that Uncle Wiggily would have more time to go riding in his automobile or his airship.

After that everything was just fine and dandy. With Nurse Jane and Cousin Betty to take care of his little rabbits, some of whom called the rabbit gentleman daddy, and some of whom called him Uncle Wiggily, jolly old

Mr. Longears could go adventuring as often as he pleased.

"La! La! La!" he would sing. "What fun I am going to find. Every day I'll be on my way for many kinds of adventures!"

One day, as Uncle Wiggily was hopping through the woods, while Nurse Jane and Cousin Betty Flufftail were in the bungalow looking after the little rabbits, the rabbit gentleman was twinkling his pink nose and wondering what adventure he might find, when, all of a sudden —

Oh, dear me! There is no room in this chapter to tell you what happened all of a sudden. But I will tell you in the next chapter if the egg beater will help the can opener to take the olives out of the gold fish bowl and make a chocolate cake for the canary bird.

Chapter 2

Circus Clown Dog

All of a sudden Uncle Wiggily heard a voice calling:

"Hurry! Hurry! Hurry! Right this way folks, for the big show! Come and see it! Hurry! Hurry! Hurry!"

"My goodness!" thought Uncle Wiggily as he came to the edge of the woods, near where a big meadow began, "that sounds like the circus elephant talking. But I didn't see any circus posters around Woodland. I didn't know the circus was coming to town. But it must be here. I'll take a look."

The jolly rabbit gentleman, twinkling his pink nose, hopped toward the meadow, for it was there he heard the calls once more:

"Hurry! Hurry! Hurry! This way to the big show! Hurry! Hurry! Hurry!"

"I don't want to be late," said Uncle Wiggily, "so I had better hurry." He hopped faster and when he finally reached the green meadow, he saw a large trailer house on wheels, such as many travelers live in.

The trailer was painted red and yellow, just like a circus wagon and in front of it, walking up and down, was a dog gentleman. The dog gentleman was dressed like a circus clown, wearing a white suit splashed with red dots and his face was painted black, white, blue, green and yellow.

"Hurry! Hurry! Hurry!" barked the circus clown dog.

"Excuse me," said Uncle Wiggily politely, "but I don't
see any circus or show. Where is it? All I see is this trailer. I
don't even see an auto to haul it along the road. Unless,"
went on the rabbit gentleman, "your circus trailer has an
auto inside it."

"No, it hasn't," and the circus clown dog spoke sadly.
"It's just a trailer. It must be pulled along by an auto as all
trailers must be pulled."

"But where is your auto?" asked Uncle Wiggily.

"It's a long, sad story," barked the dog. Then, snapping
the short whip he carried on the stiffly starched pants he
wore, the circus clown shouted again:

"Come one! Come all! Come to the big show! See the
monkey doodle boys play baseball. Hurry! Hurry! Hurry!"

14

"But where are the circus performers?" asked Uncle Wiggily. "Where is the baby elephant, where is the daring young cat on the flying trapeze who drinks bottles of milk with the greatest of ease? Where are the monkey doodle boys who play baseball? Where are they all?"

The circus clown dog said sadly:

"I wish I knew." Then he sat down on the steps of the trailer and began to cry. And as he cried the tears made the dabs of paint on his face run into streaks, circles and criss-crosses so that he looked funnier than before. "I wish I knew!" he sobbed.

"What do you wish you knew?" asked Uncle Wiggily.

"I wish I knew where all my animal circus performers are," barked the dog. "Hurry! Hurry! Hurry!" he shouted.

"But you haven't a big show," said Uncle Wiggily. "All you have is an empty trailer. Where did all the performers go? They must be some place."

"They are, I suppose," sadly sobbed the dog, "but I don't know where. All I know is that I drove my auto, hauling the trailer, to this meadow last night. We had given a show over at Frogtown, if you know where that is."

"Yes, I know where Frogtown is," said Uncle Wiggily.

"Well," went on the dog, "we parked here for the night, intending to give a show today. But when I awakened, my auto was gone. I was alone, sleeping in the trailer. I think my circus performers all ran away in the auto in the night."

"They probably did," agreed Uncle Wiggily. "But what are you going to do with a circus trailer and no auto and no performers? What are you going to do with this trailer?"

"Listen!" said the clown circus dog. "I am going to give this trailer to you, Uncle Wiggily. This is your trailer from now on. I'm going to retire. Hurry! Hurry! Hurry!"

Uncle Wiggily's nose twinkled very fast. And if the pussy dog will give the puppy cat a ride in the doll carriage down to the corner and back, I'll tell you more in the next chapter.

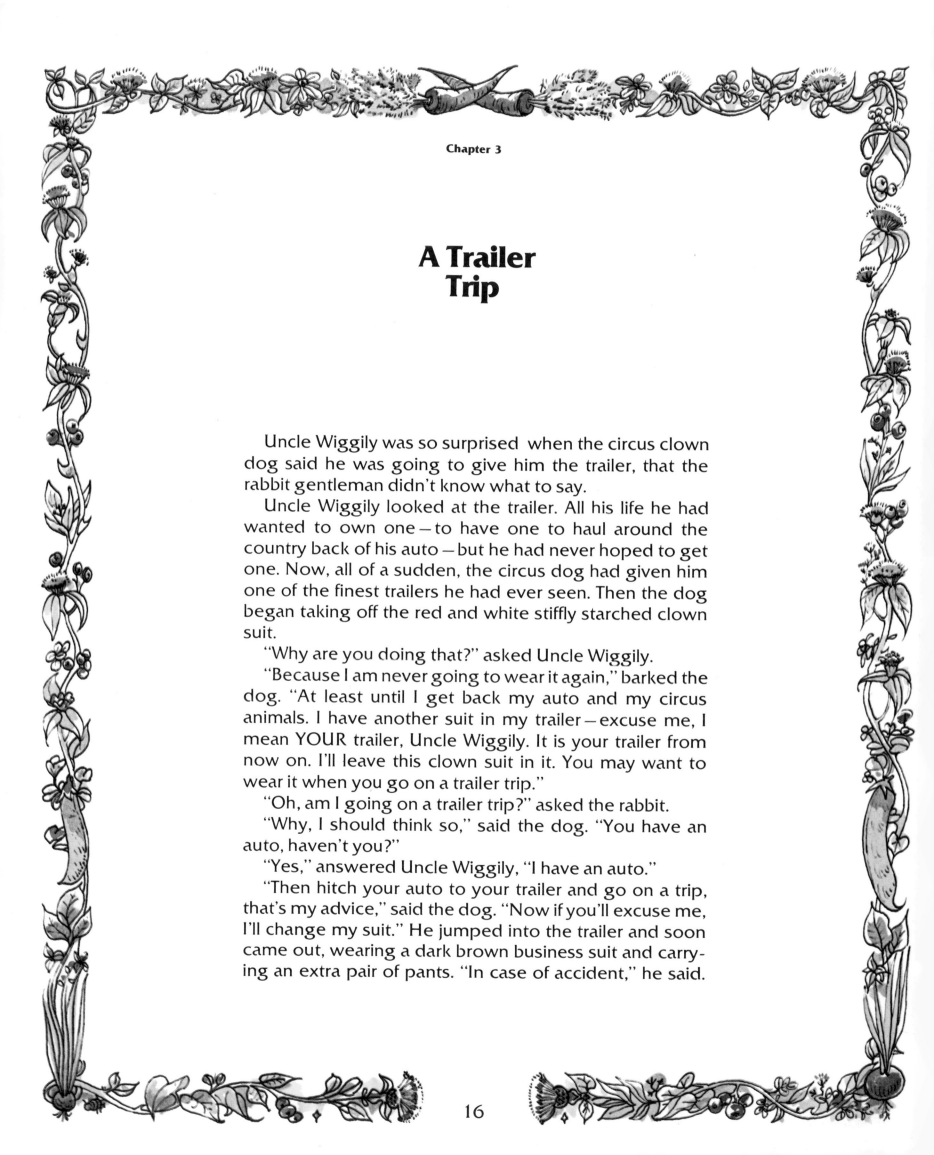

Chapter 3

A Trailer Trip

Uncle Wiggily was so surprised when the circus clown dog said he was going to give him the trailer, that the rabbit gentleman didn't know what to say.

Uncle Wiggily looked at the trailer. All his life he had wanted to own one—to have one to haul around the country back of his auto—but he had never hoped to get one. Now, all of a sudden, the circus dog had given him one of the finest trailers he had ever seen. Then the dog began taking off the red and white stiffly starched clown suit.

"Why are you doing that?" asked Uncle Wiggily.

"Because I am never going to wear it again," barked the dog. "At least until I get back my auto and my circus animals. I have another suit in my trailer—excuse me, I mean YOUR trailer, Uncle Wiggily. It is your trailer from now on. I'll leave this clown suit in it. You may want to wear it when you go on a trailer trip."

"Oh, am I going on a trailer trip?" asked the rabbit.

"Why, I should think so," said the dog. "You have an auto, haven't you?"

"Yes," answered Uncle Wiggily, "I have an auto."

"Then hitch your auto to your trailer and go on a trip, that's my advice," said the dog. "Now if you'll excuse me, I'll change my suit." He jumped into the trailer and soon came out, wearing a dark brown business suit and carrying an extra pair of pants. "In case of accident," he said.

"And now, Uncle Wiggily, I'm off. I'm going over the hill and far away. Good luck to you on your trailer trip! Good bye!"

Uncle Wiggily was hopping to his hollow stump bungalow when, all of a sudden, he heard a noise in the bushes.

"I had better hide until I see who this is," said Mr. Longears to himself. So he hid beneath a big burdock leaf and looking out, he saw only his little rabbit boy named Buster.

"Hello, Buster," called Uncle Wiggily. But he spoke so suddenly the little bunny boy jumped away up in the air and was going to hop away.

"Don't be afraid, Buster!" Uncle Wiggily called to him. "I'm not a bad chap."

"Oh, I thought, for a moment, you were," said Buster, his little heart beating very fast. "But I'm glad it's you, Uncle Wiggily. Cousin Betty sent me to look for you."

"Is anything the matter back at the hollow stump bungalow, Buster?" asked Uncle Wiggily.

"Yes," answered Buster, "there is. Cousin Betty Flufftail and Nurse Jane Fuzzy Wuzzy just had a meeting."

"What sort of meeting?" asked Mr. Longears.

"A meeting to decide where we are going this Summer vacation," Buster answered.

"And what did they decide — where are we going?" asked Uncle Wiggily.

"To the seashore," Buster replied. "So, as soon as the meeting of Cousin Betty and Nurse Jane was over, they sent me to look for you. And I've found you."

"But we shall not need my airship and an extra auto to take you all to the seashore this season, Buster," said Uncle Wiggily.

"Why not?" asked the little rabbit boy.

"Because I have a trailer," answered Mr. Longears.

"Oh, boy! A trailer? A real trailer?" shouted Buster. "Where is it, Uncle Wiggily?"

"Back in the meadow. A circus clown dog gave it to me. I'm going to haul the trailer to my bungalow. Then we'll all go to the seashore," said Mr. Longears.

He and Uncle Wiggily were soon at the hollow stump bungalow. Cousin Betty Flufftail was out in front.

"Did Buster tell you?" she asked.

19

"Yes," answered Uncle Wiggily. "And I'm in favor of the seashore."

"Wait until you see what we're going to get!" cried Buster. "It's a—"

"Hush! Don't tell! Let's surprise her!" whispered Uncle Wiggily. He hurried to get his auto from the garage.

"What are you two up to now?" asked Cousin Betty.

"You'll soon see," laughed Uncle Wiggily. "All aboard, Buster. We'll go get it!"

Cousin Betty was very much surprised. But if the jumping jack will stand on his head long enough for the shoemaker to put rubber heels on the roller skates, I'll tell you more in the next chapter.

Chapter 4

On The Beach

Uncle Wiggily was sitting at the steering wheel of his automobile, hauling the circus trailer down to the seashore. In the auto were Nurse Jane Fuzzy, Cousin Betty, and many rabbit children, including Bunty the orphan bunny.

Sitting beside Uncle Wiggily was the jolly circus clown dog who had given the rabbit gentleman the trailer because all the circus performers had run away.

"Excuse me, but this is a very funny auto you are driving and using to haul the trailer. I notice you are nibbling your turnip steering wheel."

"Oh, I often do that," laughed Mr. Longears. "I can eat my lunch and steer at the same time."

"What kind of tires have you on your auto?" asked the dog. "I was noticing them as I got in. They look odd."

"My tires are made of bologna sausages—the big kind," said Uncle Wiggily.

"Bologna sausages!" exclaimed the dog. "How odd. Why, then your auto tires are also good to eat."

"Yes," said Uncle Wiggily, "they are. But as I am a rabbit I don't eat meat. I eat only vegetables. Excuse me," he went on, "I think I had better go a little faster or we shall never reach the seashore in time," and Uncle Wiggily sprinkled some pepper over the side of the auto.

"Why did you do that?" asked the dog.

"Oh, I always do that," said the rabbit. "I sprinkle black pepper on my bologna sausage tires when I want to go fast, and if I want to go extra fast I use hot red pepper."

All of a sudden a loud, booming sound was heard.

"It's thunder!" mewed Buttercup. "I don't like it."

"That's the sound of the ocean waves," said Uncle Wiggily. "We are at the seashore. Now for adventures!"

Uncle Wiggily twisted the turnip steering wheel of his funny auto until it and the trailer were headed straight for the place whence came that booming sound.

"You can do plenty of fishing at the seashore," said Uncle Wiggily. "We'll soon be there. I think perhaps," he said, "that you and Cousin Betty and Nurse Jane would be more comfortable in a cottage. I did think we could all live in the trailer. But it will be rather a tight fit, with Boo Boo and Buttercup and so many rabbits. So I will look for a cottage and park the auto and trailer near it. Then you and I and Nurse Jane will live in the seashore cottage."

But when Uncle Wiggily tried to find a cottage to rent at the seashore, not one could be found.

"I can let you have a tent," said the real estate agent lobster who rented cottages and bungalows. "You can set the tent up on the beach, near your trailer and auto."

"That will be wonderful!" said Uncle Wiggily. "Oh, what fun and adventures I shall have here at the shore."

"And every day I'll sell popcorn and balloons on the boardwalk," barked Boo Boo. The boardwalk was near where Uncle Wiggily had set up the tent.

Early next day Boo Boo took a basket of popcorn balls and a bunch of balloons down to the boardwalk to sell.

"May I come with you?" asked Tootsie, one of Uncle Wiggily's little rabbit friends.

"Hop along," barked Boo Boo. So Tootsie hopped along. And when Boo Boo was setting up his basket of popcorn balls Tootsie asked if she might hold the bunch of balloons.

"Yes," said Boo Boo. "Hold them tight." Tootsie took the bunch of balloon cords in her paws but, all of a sudden, up in the air she went.

Tootsie the little rabbit girl went up in the air very suddenly. One moment she had been holding the bunch of balloons for Boo Boo the circus clown dog. The next moment the balloons went up in the air and Tootsie went with them.

"Oh, please get me down before I blow out to sea! Save me!"

Boo Boo was a trick circus clown. In the circus ring, wearing a white starched suit with red dots, he used to jump up in the air and shout: "Hurry! Hurry! Hurry!"

Now it was time to do that same trick, he thought.

"Only this time I must jump high enough to catch hold of Tootsie and pull her and the balloons down out of the

23

air!" barked the circus dog. "This is the time for me to hurry! Hurry! Hurry!"

Boo Boo jumped up. But he could not jump far enough to reach Tootsie. The balloons were lifting the little rabbit girl higher and higher and higher in the air.

The little rabbit girl was now floating above the boardwalk near some swings. Buttercup quickly jumped up on one of the swings and began swinging. Out and back; out and back; out and back swung the yellow cat.

"I am going to save Tootsie!" mewed the cat. She swung away out over the boardwalk; closer and closer to floating Tootsie. Then, all of a sudden, Buttercup let go her hold of the swing and went sailing through the air with the greatest of ease, like a daring young cat on the circus trapeze. Straight for Tootsie and the balloons swung Buttercup.

"Oh! Oh!" cried Tootsie as she found herself being clasped by Buttercup. "What are you going to do? Are you going to let the balloons carry you away with me?"

"No, indeed, my dear Tootsie!" mewed the circus cat. "I am just going to hold you tightly in my paws. With my weight and yours we shall be so heavy that the bunch of balloons can not hold us up. We shall float gently back to the boardwalk."

Tootsie was saved, just as Buttercup had promised.

For several weeks Uncle Wiggily and his family lived at the seashore and had lots of fun and many adventures. But, after a while, Uncle Wiggily thought it would be fun to go back to his hollow stump bungalow. I'll tell you about what happened in the next chapter if the tea kettle will please stop tickling the umbrella in the ribs to make it sneeze.

Chapter 5

The Woozie Wolf

Uncle Wiggily was in the middle of the log bridge over the woodland brook when he heard that rustling noise in the bushes behind him. The rabbit gentleman turned so quickly, to see what had made the noise, that he nearly slipped off the log into the water.

But he didn't quite fall and so, balancing himself with the greatest of ease, like Buttercup on the flying trapeze, Uncle Wiggily looked back along the shore of the brook.

To his glad surprise, out of the bushes hopped his little friend Pricklie Porky, the porcupine boy. Pricklie's long, sharp quills, as pointed as arrows, were sticking out every which-way from his back and sides. They rattled in the wind, for the quills of a porcupine are as hard as wooden toothpicks and much sharper.

"Oh, so it's you, is it, Uncle Wiggily?" asked Pricklie.

"Yes," answered the rabbit gentleman, "it is. And I am glad to see you instead of a bad chap. I just met one of them."

Just then, there was a rustling in the trees over the heads of Mr. Longears and Pricklie Porky. Uncle Wiggily had walked back over the log bridge and was now on the same side of the brook as was the porcupine boy.

"What's that noise?" asked Pricklie.

"I hope it was only the wind," said Uncle Wiggily. "I hope it isn't the Bobcat coming back. At first, as I was in the middle of the log bridge, I heard this rustling noise in the bushes and I thought you might be the Bobcat."

26

"If it was the Bobcat, I guess Pricklie Porky would have shot him full of his sharp quill arrows," said another voice.

"Who are you?" asked Uncle Wiggily in surprise.

"I am Johnnie Bushytail, up in the tree over your head," was the chattering answer.

Unlike Tommie, Joie or Kittie Kat, the squirrel boy could come down the tree head first. When a cat climbs a tree he goes up head first and then backs down tail first. That's the way of cats.

"Yes," went on Johnnie as he found part of a last year's acorn which he nibbled, "I guess you are glad I wasn't a bad chap, or you might have shot your arrow quills at me, Pricklie Porky."

"Now that's where you are wrong," said Uncle Wiggily. "Give Johnnie a little nature lesson, my little stickery friend."

"We porcupines can't shoot our quills like arrows," said Pricklie. "Our quills are fastened in our skin and fur very loosely. They will stick in anybody who touches them and will come loose. And my quills have barbs on the end, like the barbs on fish hooks. So when my quills stick in any-body, they pull out of my fur so easily that it almost seems as if I shot the quills. But I don't."

"Sometimes I use my tail," said Pricklie. "My tail is like a club. It has a lot of loose quills on it. And when I lash about with my tail, and hit a bad chap on the nose, his nose gets stuck full of my little quill arrows."

"I should think," said Johnnie, "that after a while you would have no more quills left."

"Oh, my quills grow in again," said the little porcupine boy.

"Just like the hairs in your bushy tail, Johnnie," explained Uncle Wiggily.

28

"Thank you for telling me so much about nature," spoke the little boy squirrel. "I have learned so much I think I need never go back to school again."

Johnnie scampered back home. Uncle Wiggily and Pricklie Porky crossed the log bridge over the brook and walked together in the fields and through the woods.

"Do you mind if I come adventuring with you, Uncle Wiggily?" asked the little porcupine boy.

"I am delighted to have you," said the rabbit gentleman. "I was getting lonesome."

"Anyhow, you know I promised to be a sort of protector to you," went on Pricklie. "If any bad chaps come after you I will strike them with my tail and fill them full of quills."

"I'm sure you will," said Uncle Wiggily. "But I don't believe I will meet any more bad chaps today."

29

Over the fields and through the woods they wandered. All of a sudden, as they were going down a little hill, into a dingly dell, Uncle Wiggily stopped and said:

"Oh! Oh!"

"What's the matter?" asked the porcupine boy.

"The Wolf is coming," said Uncle Wiggily. "He is heading right this way. Oh, dear me! I dare not run for he would soon catch me and pounce on me. What shall I do?"

"Leave it to me," said Pricklie. "I promised to protect you from all bad chaps. Let the Wolf come! I dare him!"

And on came the Wolf, his tongue hanging hungrily out of his red mouth. Uncle Wiggily felt so unhappy he couldn't twinkle his pink nose.

But don't worry. Everything is going to be fine and dandy in the next chapter if the cabbage will please stop standing on its head and turning somersaults over the bottle of vinegar to make the coffee pot laugh.

Chapter 6

The Fuzzie Fox

Before the Wolf reached the place in the dingly dell, or little meadow hollow, where Uncle Wiggily and Pricklie Porky waited, the little porcupine boy whispered:

"Listen to me, Uncle Wiggily. The wolf is too big and strong for either of us to fight him. We must fool him. You will soon see," said Pricklie. "Just do as I tell you, please.

Along came slithering the hungry Wolf.

"Good morning, Uncle Wiggily," snarled the bad chap, pretending to be polite, which he wasn't in the least.

"Bad morning you mean," said Uncle Wiggily. "At least it's bad for me."

"It's good for me!" chuckled the Wolf. "Now let me see, which ear shall I nibble first? Um! Ah! I think I'll try the left ear."

"Oh, no, please don't!" begged Uncle Wiggily.

"O.K.! I won't. I've changed my mind. I'll nibble your right ear first, it seems a bit fatter than the left. Will you please bend over a little so I can get at you better? Now for the right ear. Ah, ha!" growled the Wolf.

"But let me ask you a question," said Uncle Wiggily.

"Go ahead, ask it," snarled the Wolf. "But be quick about it."

"Are you a good, high kicker?" asked the rabbit.

"I'm one of the highest kickers in the woods," boasted the Wolf.

"Can you kick higher than I can kick?" asked the jolly old rabbit gentleman.

"Of course I can kick higher than you!" snarled the bad chap. "Fooie on your kicking! Let's see you give a kick, and if I can't kick twice as high as you, well—but no matter. Go ahead—kick!"

"One! Two! Three!" counted Mr. Longears. He kicked up in the air toward the Wolf, as if he were about to kick the ragged cap off the bad chap's head. But Uncle Wiggily's kick went only about as high as the middle button on the Wolf's coat.

"Ha! Ha!" laughed Woozie Wolf. "If I couldn't kick any better than that I'd play ping pong instead of football! Now watch me!"

But, just as the Wolf kicked, Uncle Wiggily hopped to one side and Pricklie Porky rolled himself down in front of the bad chap. So that the Wolf, instead of kicking off Uncle Wiggily's hat, or even kicking into the air, kicked with all his might right on the sharp, pointed spiny quills of Pricklie Porky!

"Wham!"

What a kick it was!

Of course Pricklie was kicked up in the air like a football, but he knew he wouldn't get hurt when he fell down, for his fur full of quills was like a padded football suit.

And then, all of a quickness, the Wolf danced around on his left hind leg. And he held his right hind leg in his two front paws and he howled, and he yowled and he scowled.

"Oh, zowie! Oh, zoozie! Oh, pin cushions and cheese graters!" howled Woozie Wolf. "What did I kick?"

"You kicked Pricklie Porky, my little porcupine protector!" shouted Uncle Wiggily. "Do you want to kick him again?"

"I do NOT!" howled the Wolf. And away he limped far off in the woods.

And then, on the wind, the voice of the Wolf came back to the two friends.

"Just you wait!" threatened the bad chap. "I'll tell Fuzzie Fox on you, that's what I'll do. He'll nibble your ears, Mr. Uncle Wiggily! Just you wait! I'll tell Fuzzie Fox!"

"Fooie!" shouted Pricklie. "I don't believe I need protect you any more, Mr. Longears. So I'll be on my way. See you later. Happy days!"

Uncle Wiggily hopped on and on. In a little while, he reached a sort of bosky dell in the woods where some wild turkeys used to live before Thanksgiving. They roosted in trees and the ground beneath the trees was covered with loose turkey feathers.

"Ha! I'm glad I found these," said Uncle Wiggily. "Buster was asking me to bring him some feathers. He is going to dress up like an Indian. I'll pick up a lot of these turkey feathers and bring them home to Buster."

So, carrying the bark basket of feathers on one paw, along the woodland path the rabbit gentleman hopped until, all of a sudden, something happened.

Out of a clump of bushes jumped Fuzzie Fox.

"Oh, dear me!" exclaimed Uncle Wiggily and his pink nose twinkled very fast.

But have no fears. Something funny is going to happen in the next chapter. If the front door mat will go around and play tag with the back steps and the clothes posts so the kitchen sink will not be lonesome, I'll tell you all about it.

Chapter 7

A Big Surprise

Fuzzie Fox looked at Uncle Wiggily. Fuzzie Fox rubbed his red tongue over his white teeth in a hungry way and said:

"Oh, here you are, my rabbit lunch!"

"Yes, here I am, but I wish I were somewhere else," said Mr. Longears. "But what did you call me, Fuzzie Fox?"

"I called you my rabbit lunch," answered the bad chap.

"May I ask why?" inquired Uncle Wiggily. He thought that if he talked to the Fox long enough the Police Dog might come along and arrest the bad chap.

"The reason I called you my rabbit lunch, Mr. Longears," said the Fox in a yapping voice, "is that you are a rabbit, aren't you?"

"Yes," answered Uncle Wiggily, "I am a rabbit."

"And you are going to be my lunch," went on Fuzzie Fox. "Now you know why I called you my rabbit lunch."

He softly stepped closer to the rabbit gentleman and then, all of sudden, he stopped and looked at what Uncle Wiggily was carrying.

At first Mr. Longears thought the Fox saw the Police Dog coming to the rescue. But the rabbit gentleman knew differently when the Fox said:

"I see you have a turkey with you."

"Oh, yes, you see turkey feathers all right," admitted Uncle Wiggily. He wasn't going to tell a story. He really had turkey feathers in the birch bark basket. But the feathers were for Buster to play Indian with. There was no turkey.

"I am very fond of turkey," went on Fuzzie Fox. "I can eat turkey at any time. I don't have to wait for Thanksgiving or Christmas. Every day is turkey day for me—when I can get a turkey. And I am going to get one now."

With that the Fox snatched the bark basket of turkey feathers from Uncle Wiggily's paw and away ran Fuzzie Fox with it over the hill and far away, thinking he had a turkey.

"Yes, I have had adventures enough this happy, Summer day. I shall hop home as fast as I can," said the jolly rabbit.

Uncle Wiggily hopped over the fields and through the woods to his hollow stump bungalow.

Fuzzie Fox, chuckling to himself over the feast he thought he was going to have, ran home to his den in the rocks. He set the basket of turkey feathers (which he thought was a real turkey) down on the floor of his den. Then he went to the telephone, for even animal bad chaps sometimes have telephones in their dens. The Fox called up the Bobcat.

"Hello, Bobbie!" spoke the Fox, when the other bad chap answered the telephone. "I have a big surprise for you, Bobbie! A turkey surprise. Come on over to my den," yapped the Fox.

"I'll be there before you can pick the wish bone," said the Bobcat.

Next the Fox called Woozie Wolf.

"Hello, Wolfie!" spoke the Fox over the telephone. "I have a surprise for you. A turkey surprise. Come on over to my den. Bobbie Cat is coming. We'll have a party. Hurry!" said the Fox. "Hurry!"

"I'll come as soon as I can," answered the Wolf. "But I can't hurry."

"Why not?" asked the Fox.

"Because I have some – er – some – um – some splinters in my paw," growled the Wolf. He didn't want to tell how he had been fooled and how he kicked Pricklie Porky and so got the porcupine quills in his paw.

"I'll come as fast as I can," said the Wolf. "Save some of the white meat of the turkey for me."

"I will," promised the Fox. "But hurry! Bobbie Cat and I will be waiting for you."

First to reach the den of the Fox was the Bobcat.

"Where's the turkey?" he mewed.

"There," said the Fox pointing to the bark basket of feathers. "I haven't started to cook it yet."

There was a noise outside the den of the Fox.

"Maybe this is Wolfie," said the Bobcat.

"Yes, it is," said the Fox as he looked out. "How are you, Wolfie?"

"Oh, not so very well," answered Woozie Wolf. He came in limping.

"What's the matter?" asked the Bobcat.

"Oh—I—er—I sort of stepped on a tack," growled the Wolf.

"I thought you told me you had splinters in your paw," said the Fox, suspicious like and distrustful.

39

"Oh, well, what odds?" snarled the Wolf. "Let's see this wonderful turkey, Foxie."

"Here it is," said the Fox, picking up the basket of feathers. "Aren't you chaps surprised at how smart I am? I took this turkey from Uncle Wiggily."

Woozie Wolf reached into the basket. Of course all he picked up was a pawful of loose turkey feathers.

"Look! Look!" howled the Wolf. "Turkey? Turkey? Why it's only FEATHERS! Bah!"

"Oh, what a surprise!" moaned Fuzzie Fox.

"**I sho**uld say it was!" mewed the Bobcat. "A BIG surprise!"

Do you want to know what happened next? Well, please turn to the next chapter which you may read if the radio doesn't talk in its sleep and make the alarm clock ring before breakfast time.

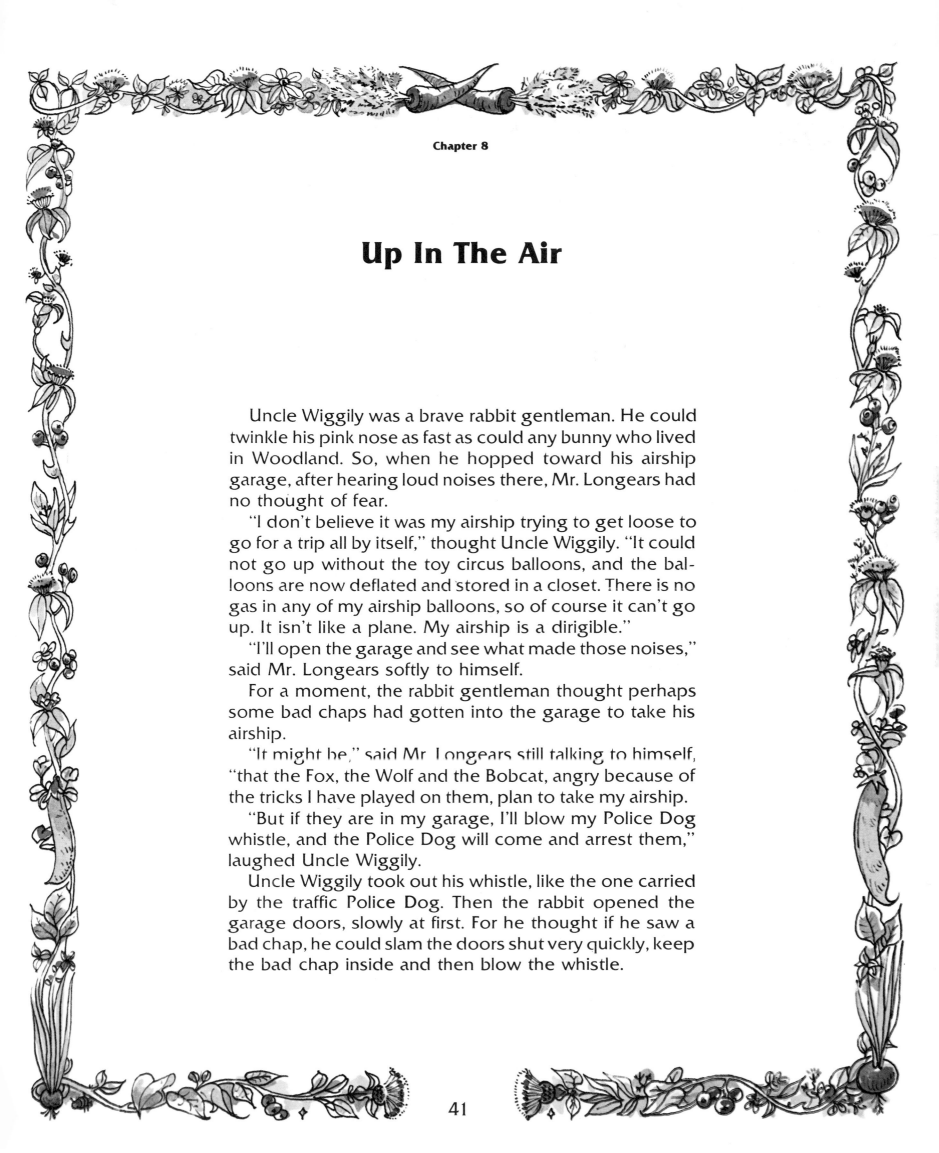

Chapter 8

Up In The Air

Uncle Wiggily was a brave rabbit gentleman. He could twinkle his pink nose as fast as could any bunny who lived in Woodland. So, when he hopped toward his airship garage, after hearing loud noises there, Mr. Longears had no thought of fear.

"I don't believe it was my airship trying to get loose to go for a trip all by itself," thought Uncle Wiggily. "It could not go up without the toy circus balloons, and the balloons are now deflated and stored in a closet. There is no gas in any of my airship balloons, so of course it can't go up. It isn't like a plane. My airship is a dirigible."

"I'll open the garage and see what made those noises," said Mr. Longears softly to himself.

For a moment, the rabbit gentleman thought perhaps some bad chaps had gotten into the garage to take his airship.

"It might be," said Mr. Longears still talking to himself, "that the Fox, the Wolf and the Bobcat, angry because of the tricks I have played on them, plan to take my airship.

"But if they are in my garage, I'll blow my Police Dog whistle, and the Police Dog will come and arrest them," laughed Uncle Wiggily.

Uncle Wiggily took out his whistle, like the one carried by the traffic Police Dog. Then the rabbit opened the garage doors, slowly at first. For he thought if he saw a bad chap, he could slam the doors shut very quickly, keep the bad chap inside and then blow the whistle.

All was now quiet inside the garage. Not a sound was heard. Uncle Wiggily opened the doors a little wider. He looked in. He saw no bad chaps at all.

"I must have been mistaken," said the jolly old rabbit gentleman. "What I heard was the Summer wind blowing. I'm glad no bad chaps are here."

Then as he looked at his airship, Uncle Wiggily had a sudden idea.

"I will go for a little trip!" he said.

As I promised to tell you, the rabbit gentleman's airship was a queer one. It was made from a big clothes basket. To make it lift itself up into the air, Uncle Wiggily would fasten on the basket several toy, circus balloons filled with gas from the swamp near his bungalow.

To make the airship sail ahead, after it was up in the air, Uncle Wiggily had, at the back of the clothes basket, an electric fan turned by a small gasoline engine.

To steer his ship from side to side, and to slant it up or
down, after the toy circus balloons had lifted it into the air,
Uncle Wiggily used old tin tea trays that Nurse Jane Fuzzy
Wuzzy had given him. The trays were fastened to the
sides and to the back of the airship. To the trays were tied
long strings which were within easy reach of the rabbit
pilot as he sat behind the baby carriage steering wheel.

Piled in the clothes basket were many soft sofa cushions. In case of a crash landing, or if Uncle Wiggily had to
come to the ground suddenly, these sofa cushions made
a soft place on which he could fall.

"Now I am ready to take a trip and spend some happy
days. I will put some gasoline in the motor to spin the
electric fan propeller. Then I will put some gas in the
balloons to fill them out and lift up my airship."

Not far from Uncle Wiggily's bungalow was a marsh, or swamp. There, a gas was made from decayed and rotten grass, leaves and wood. Sometimes, at night, this marsh gas would become lighted. Then, in the dark, it would glow like a candle in a Jack o' Lantern. In some places this lighted marsh gas is called Will o' The Wisp, or Fox Fire. It has the Latin name of Ignus Fatuus. Persons who don't know what causes it are frightened when they see it in a swamp.

When he had enough inflated balloons on his ship to make it float but not go up in the air, Uncle Wiggily moved the craft out of the garage into the yard. There he anchored it to a clothes post. Next he fastened on the last of the gas balloons. By this time the airship was pulling and tugging at the anchor rope, eager and anxious to get away.

"All aboard!" cried the rabbit pilot. He jumped into the

clothes basket. He stepped on the starter of the engine. The electric fan began to whizz. Uncle Wiggily held the steering wheel firmly. Then he cut the anchor rope.

Up shot the ship. Uncle Wiggily tilted a tea tray and his ship slanted toward the clouds.

"Here I go! Happy days!" shouted Uncle Wiggily. Up he rose, higher and higher. "I know where I am going to spend part of my happy vacation days. I wonder I didn't think of it before. Yes, I'll go there!"

Do you wonder where Uncle Wiggily is going? Well, if the pussy cat will wash the face of the clock with the end of her tail, and not tickle it so that it sneezes its hands off, I will tell you all about where Uncle Wiggily is going in the next chapter.

Oh, my goodness! There isn't going to be any next chapter, is there? We have come to the end of this book. I hope you like it, for, if you did, perhaps I can write another.

Trailer in
the meadow

Betsy
Flufftail's
burrow

To Post
OFFICE

Log bridge

Swampy
place